Disclaimer

This is a work of fiction. Any names, businesses, characters, events, incidents and places are either the product of the author's imagination or used in a fictitious manner. Any resemblance to actual people, living or dead, or actual events or occurrences is purely coincidental.

Holy Paladin's Quest

The Angel's Blessing
Book 1

By Blaine Hart
Copyright © 2016

Check Out all My Books and Audio Books at: www.LordHartRules.com

Table of Contents

Chapter 1: The Day of the White Rook

My Master did not become the great Warrior Shaman of peace because he was born with the blessings of the gods. He did not rise to his exalted place in the history of our worlds by the chance of ancestry, nor was he a child of fortune. He had no advantage other than his cunning, and he had no blessing other than that given to him by his grandfather. And that blessing was herb-lore.

My master was conceived and born in violence.

His mother was a young beauty who was ravaged by the invading Veylus pirates when our beloved city of Barnacle Atoll was overrun. When her time to give birth came, she held the newborn infant to her breast, the scrawny infant seeking to suckle a tit. But the nipple that the child found was cold and so he turned to his grandfather's thumb instead, and that thumb was hard and calloused and yet rich with the taste of mother-earth and her herbs. And so in his first suckle of life, the babe that was to be known simply as Kell, tasted the roots of us all.

Kell spent his youngest years under the domination of the brigands, and he quickly learned stealth and cunning as a way of life. In time, the Veylus were ousted by the armada of Queen Anastasias, and while her liberation was near devastation, the people of the Barnacles were once again free. With that freedom came years of reconstruction and tribute to the Queen, but that was far better than the pirates.

In that time Kell grew up as boys will. He was astounded with the world. His grandfather had a bountiful garden, and in there Kell saw crawlers and wigglers and flyers of all sorts. As a toddler, he tasted them and found them much crunchier than the wiggly ones of the root cellar. His grandfather often looked at him and sighed as adults will. But despite his odd tastes, he grew up healthy and strong.

Their small island of Dunsil wasn't on many sea-routes, but he and his grandfather were often visited by passing ships looking for a remedy to help a wounded or sick crewman. Often a boatful of sailors would come ashore and seek one of grandfather's special elixirs, and then ask of the ways with which to work the earth's gift. His grandfather never refused anyone in need -- for a fair price. Over the years, the legends grew of his incredible remedies. It was an ideal childhood and Kell was very happy.

Until the day that the Dorimans engulfed their island.

They were a gang of thugs with ships. Their fleet was small and fast and they would prey on defenseless lands, not to conquer, but to plunder and destroy. And before the Queen's forces could come to aid, they would sail away into the night's fog only to reappear in some other land, rough-handed and demanding. They wore no uniforms, and in their motley gear Kell saw them as something to be afraid of. He was a teenager at the time and the Dorimans saw him as a value to their number. And so at his grandfather's urging, he drew on all his cunning and he ran away.

He ran across the crest of the island and to the common ground where others were also gathering and afraid. Understanding his plight, the elders brought him to a cove with a light boat hidden within. They told him to sail straight to Angove's Cay, which was the home of Wendfala the Witch.

The young witch, seeing my Master's comely and youthful state, took him in and proceeded to teach him the ancient ways. It is said that in those dark hours while our very island writhed beneath the boots of the Dorimans, Wendfala made my Master into a man, and the young boy emerged from her clutches alert, able and with a new sort of strength that radiated off him like an aura.

They say that he emerged from her embraces as a magical paladin who single-handedly rallied the people and sent the Dorimans howling away and afraid. They say that he was the hero who liberated our islands and that the Doriman still fear his name. And they say that when he was done with the Dorimans, the of battle was still upon him, and so he sailed the world in search of glory, wisdom and to inflict Holy Justice upon the wicked. For years sailors and merchants would land on our island and tell tales of Kell's valor in lands unknown.

That's what they say.

In the years of peace that followed many tales were told and retold, and then told and changed again and again. And in the small confines of the island of Dunsil the simple herbalist's grandchild became a living legend.

He returned to our island the year that I was born, and while many looked at the legendary hero in awe, their real amazement was that the lad looked as if he had never left. It was as though time had not touched him, and when he walked into his grandfather's cottage with his backpack full of magic and treasures, the old man simply looked up and told him that the garden needed tending.

He would say nothing of his adventures, but people would talk. Kell shunned their stories, but he didn't shun their company. He was still young and he had a quick wit at the tavern and loved winning at darts and skittles. The young women all eyed him and so at the festivals and dances he never lacked a partner. His knowledge of herbs and medicines grew as his grandfather taught him all he knew as he waned in years. People came to trust the young man as they did his old grandfather, sometimes more.

In time, the great herbalist finally passed. Every man woman and child on Dunsil stood on the white sands of the island's eastern shore as Kell made ready the last boat. They covered his body in beautiful flower blossoms, in hopes that the sea would pause and delight in the scent and so allow fair winds to carry him to his eternal paradise. Even the witch Wendfala came to give her blessing.

I was just a small boy at the time. I remember my mother urging me, my sisters and my brothers to let go of our flowers. But I was fascinated by the naked old man. He was nothing but old bones wrapped in tan skin at the bottom of a small rustic boat, and yet the blossoms made him seem almost alive.

"Forgive my child Kell," my mother said. "He is –"

"Young," Kell said. "And fascinated."

Then he set his gaze on me and he smiled.

It was not that long after the funeral that I was selected to be Kell's apprentice. I trembled with the honor and surged with excitement.

I had heard all of the grand tales. Indeed, I had been raised in the shadow of those magnificent stories, and when he and my father bartered for my apprenticeship, I thought that the gods themselves had blessed me.

"He's kind of scrawny."

"Yeah," my father said. "He is. But how much bulk do you need to scratch out your herbs?"

Kell frowned.

"Look," my father said. "I have a farm. Farming is a strong man's job. The boy will be better in your hands. I will give you milk, cheese and all the whey you want for four years."

"Seven."

I listened as they haggled over my worth. In the end I went for the price of six years of milk, three of cheeses and all the whey I could carry between the houses until I was seventeen.

It was a good bargain.

Master Kell was a soft-spoken and kindly man. He treated me well and our house wanted for nothing. Along with teaching me herb lore, he also taught me numbers and letters, and while I found numbers valuable in weighing and mixing and figuring out the price to put on a remedy, I never understood why Kell put so much value on writing.

We worked in a daily routine and there were always things to get done or learn. But Kell was a light-hearted soul and we often took the time to play. We would sometimes end a long day frolicking and fishing on one side of Crystal Lake while the women washed their laundry on the other. My master had an eye for the ladies and there were quite a few nights that I spent alone sleeping under the Starlight.

When I came into my teenage years I learned two very important lessons of life. One was girls. When I was young girls were simply giggly playmates, but as I matured I began to see those gigglers grow round, soft and firm, and that made me wonder. And there were odd things about my own body that I didn't understand; strange stirrings and desires. I asked my master about these feelings but he seemed somewhat at a loss, then smiled and assured me that all would be revealed in time.

I wondered about how long that time might be. And then one day a woman named Loleena came calling. She was from the other side of the island and I barely knew her. Kell graciously invited her to sup with us and the woman seemed to take an immediate interest in me. I was flattered that such a fine lady would even recognize my existence, let along talk with me.

The night was cool and getting cooler. Kell excused himself to gather more wood for the fire, but he didn't return till dawn. And that night Loleena helped me understand what it was like to be a man.

Over time I became an expert at herb lore and my master's special elixirs where in high demand, giving me plenty of practice at the craft. When it came time for the harvest festival, I was invited for the first time to join the adults around the big bonfire. There was music and dancing, and everyone cheered when Kell produced a keg of his special brew. The draught was sweet and heady and at first I didn't feel its effects. But then the festival started to feel a lot more happier to me. The dancing was lighter, the music was sweeter, and the young girls seemed prettier. The brew seemed to have the same effect on the girls as well, because they suddenly found me handsome. I did not lack for sweet company all that day and night.

Winters on the Atoll were usually cold and dreary. Work still needed to be done, but the sun would set earlier and earlier and the nights cooped up in the cottage could be wearisome. In those days I was glad to have learned my letters. My master had books on his craft and a boring volume entitled *The List of Leaves* that helped pass the dreary time.

We woke one chill sunny morning to a racket outside. Rooks were calling and crying. We rushed outside to see what was happening and the sky was nearly blotted out by their numbers. It was an amazing sight. Thousands of them were circling overhead. They seemed to be whirling in a vortex that narrowed closer and closer to the center eye, and in that eye I saw a single speck of white.

As we watched the birds became more and more frantic. The center mass of birds began to dip down and then formed into a funnel. I cried out and fell back to shield myself, but when they were only a few hundred feet above us a single rook parted from the myriad, spread its massive wings and began to descend. As it got closer we could see that the rook was as white as snow.

The pearlescent feathers seemed almost to gleam and its beak was like polished marble, but even as its spiny claws touched the sand of the earth the creature transformed. There stood before us a tall, bald man with skin as black as the night that seemed to almost shine blue where the sunlight fell on it. He was hairless from his head to his eyebrows and everywhere else a man should have hair. But what truly astonished me was that there was no manhood. At the place where his thighs met his pelvis there was nothing but smooth dark flesh.

"You are Kell," the man said in a silky, almost liquid voice.

"I am."

And for all of my amazement and growing fear my master was as calm as the sea on a spring morning.

"I am an emissary from Wendfala," he said. "The Witch calls on your pledge."

There was a long pause before my master spoke. The birds above had wheeled out in a huge circle letting the sun shine onto us.

"Why doesn't Wendfala come herself to call on this sacred pledge?" Kell asked in a powerful voice.

"She has been kidnapped," the man-bird said.

"Kidnapped?" Kell bellowed, his hand unconsciously flexing as if to grab his weapon.

"She needs your help. In fact the whole of the Nine domains need your help."

"With what? What is going on?" Kell asked with obvious concern in his voice.

"Wendfala calls for you. It's not for me to judge her choice. I am only a messenger and ask you to hear her plea. I see smoke from your chimney. Can we go inside? It's cold out here without feathers."

"Um, sure. But first tell me, what is your name?" said Kell

"I am Byrinius."

Kell motioned towards his house and as they turned to go inside Byrinius pointed towards me and asked who I was.

"This is Longo Nonan," Kell said. "He is my apprentice."

"Longo," the man said. "Look at me boy. I have no hair and I have nothing where a human male should have something. But can you tell me what else there is about me that is not like you?"

At first I was frightened and my brain refused to work. But it felt as though the two would stare at me until I either flushed or fumbled like a child, or I solved the riddle. I looked. Then I looked again, and then I saw, but the words would not form and so I simply pointed to my belly.

"That's right," Byrinius said laughing long and hard. "I have no naval. I was not born, I was hatched. Kell, the lad is astute. Let him come with us and listen."

My master gave me a strange look, but I went with them and sat quietly in the corner. Kell offered tea but the man refused. He plucked a large ember from the fire, sat at the table, and held the glowing thing in his palm as he spoke.

"Visalth is coming," the man said.

As he spoke, vapors rose from the glowing ember. The smoke grew a little and then began to spin, then gather and spread into a wide sphere, and in the center of the sphere an image began to form. It was the image of a giant skeletal Dragon... A Bone Dragon.

I had heard of such things in stories, and in my youth they were terrifying. The mindless, soulless things would always seek to steal, kill and destroy and they could listen to no reason and had no fear for their own lives.

But these were modern times. Such myths were put away long ago along with frost fairies and trolls.

But that day my eyes had seen a bird transform into the vestige of a man who was now holding a scorching cinder in his hand as if it were a pebble, and the vision that formed in the room made me believe.

The dragon's bones were not like the white bleached things of men I had seen washed up on the beaches. They were deep brown like rotten teeth. It's long skull was swept back, flaring out into nine horns that turned forward like barbed fish-hooks. The hollow orbits were long, narrow and without eyes. It had a look of evil about it. I could not count the many spike-tipped vertebrae of the creature's neck, but the thing could wind and twist like a snake. Its ribs were slender, but what once had been the torso was long. Its fore-limbs grew from a solid breast-plate that looked scarred and beaten, and they were like a man's arms ending in grasping fingers. Its massive hind-legs bent like a deer, but the thighs could have been as thick as a trader ship's mast, and the claws could have crushed our house. The wings that sprouted from its back spread like enormous bird fingers, but between those bones there was no skin, only what looked like remnants of tattered sails or the clinging bits of flesh from creatures undreamed. The tail of the beast was easily as long as the whole creature, and as I watched the dragon fly about in the vision, the bony tail would whip back between the wings to attack like a scorpion.

"Magnificent," Kell said. "Truly a feat of powerful magic."

"Dark magic," Byrinius replied.

We watched the scene as the dragon lay waste to a solid castle set on a hill. The land was unknown to me. It was a lush place with rolling green grass, well cultivated farm land surrounded by walls and then a deep forest. But as we watched, the beast seemed to delight in wreaking ruin on the castle walls and buildings. An army of warriors looked helpless against the skeletal foe. Their arrows and bolts would bounce off the bones or sail through the empty spaces of its ribs. Even the catapults the men managed to muster had little effect, and they were quickly destroyed. When the undead horror had reduced the defenses to rubble it then turned on the army, sweeping men and cavalry away with its deadly tail.

"It seems bent on wanton destruction," Kell said.

"Not so. There is method in its madness. Observe."

I watched with a dull growing terror. When the army had been broken and the warriors were fleeing, men began to march in from the woods. The dragon seemed to suddenly heed some sort of call. It lifted and flew up on wings that were no wings, circling the walled city as the invaders easily took over.

"What are we seeing?" Kell asked. "What place is this?"

"It's Breakstone Hold, the Castle of Duke Venyez in Estile."

"Estile? That's in the Nine."

"It is," the man said. "It is on the Queen's western realms. The bone dragon's name is Visalth, and it's forces seem to be working their way along the alliance. Before Estile, the Duchy of Halnn fell. But the curious thing about the invasion is the pattern of assault. There is no warning, but just before an invasion all magic seems to disappear."

"What?"

"Wizards," the man went on, "witches, mages, even holy paladins seem to disappear. Whether these are physical or spiritual abductions I cannot say. But I do know that when Visalth appears there are none who can stand before him — they all disappear or get destroyed. And now Wendfala is captured, and from her prison she sends me to you ahead of the storm to get your aid."

Kell gulped his tea. The mystical scene vanished but Byrinius still held the glowing ember. My master stood and paced the room. He ran his fingers through his hair again and again. Then he finally stood before the window and gazed out to sea. He stood a long time. He then seemed decisive and strode to a locked wardrobe. He held his fingers over the handle and mumbled a quick verse. The doors popped open and from the inside he drew out a long and stout war-hammer that was glowing brightly.

The weapon was easily as long as my arm. Its handle was wrapped with red leather that showed stains of wear and sweat. The oaken shaft was carved in a hexagon. Cold blue steel ran from the crown down that shaft and was bolted with iron. The broad, flat head could easily have crushed an Ogres Skull, and the opposite side of the hammer was a nasty six sided piece of magical steel ending in a sharp point. The pommel was thick and ended with an 8 inch long double-bladed knife made of Admantium with a magically sharpened blade. Kell tossed his trusty weapon onto the table and the weight of it shook the table and dented it in several places.

"This is my little friend Ashrune," my master said. "How might we help?"

"You need to Flee this place." Byrinius said in a grave and urgent tone.

"Never! I will not run when my Queen's lands are in danger. I am no coward." Kell bellowed, outrage in his voice.

"Bravery in the face of such a monster is suicide," Byrinius said calmly. "The power behind Visalth is cunning, and so you must be just as crafty. Ashrune may be a noble weapon but even with the might of a Titan behind, it would barely scratch the creature's skull before you were impaled. You need something far mightier, and to find such a thing you need help that is beyond simple magic. You need an Angel."

Chapter 2: The Annas

Kell and Byrinius spoke into the evening, talking of things and places that baffled me. During that time the crows whirled in the sky above, seeming anxious. The next day Byrinius returned to his bird form while dozens of folk gathered on the hill and along the wood line, silent and staring. They watched in awe as the spectacle of birds wheeled away into the morning sunrise, leaving a chilling silence in their wake.

"What does it all mean?" someone called from the crowd.

"For you," Kell said with a shrug, "nothing." But I distinctly heard him mutter "for now" under his breath.

But the people didn't like that answer.

"For me," he continued. "It means I need a boat. Wendfala is in danger. The witch needs my help, and I cannot say no. So, I need a boat. Will anyone help me?"

Two men and a woman stepped forward. One man and the woman began asking questions like "for how long?" and "how far will you need to sail?" and "how many will travel?" and "are you a good hand with a sloop?" Kell could answer none of their questions for sure other than to say that he was a fair hand at sea. That was when a third man stood forward.

"I can help you Kell," he said with a strange sort of smile.

We didn't know him, but I had seen him. He was from our atoll on an island west of Greed. He traded for our good cordage and was ashore for just that when he saw and so followed the birds.

"I have the perfect boat for you," he went on. "It's an old wreck that washed up in a tide pool by my house. I have been using it all these years as a teaching tool for my sister's children. They've been refurbishing it stem to stern, and a right good work they've made of it. It's a lusty little yawl and they have her in fair trim. The two have come of age and are eager to seek their fortunes in the world. They would be most eager to crew for you. Take them and the boat with my blessings."

The man spat on his hand and held it out. I could see that Kell was wary. But I also knew that the price was right and his needs pressed. Still, he hesitated.

"If the yawl is as fair as you say," he said. "Why wouldn't you try and sell it?"

"Naw," the man said shaking his head. "It's the children's by right, and like I say they mean to see the world. The problem is that they don't know where to start. You give 'em a mission and they'll do you well. And when you are done helping Wendfala you'll have given 'em a good launch into life. It's like they say in Merica, 'a win-win'."

Kell chuckled and shook his head. Then he spat on his hand and shook the sailor's hand. The man's smile was beaming. Kell was eager to set sail and so it was agreed that the boat would be ready and at Nillan's wharf by the noon tide in two days.

"What's the boat's name," Kell asked. "And how will I know her?"

"Oh you'll know her alright," the man smiled. "She's baby-blue above the waterline and she has lightish pink sails -- with yellow rigging."

My master and I looked at the man.

"It was the kid's doing," he said. "Clever little buggers I will say. Oh, and they named her *Chaos*. Fair winds, my friends."

The sailor nearly skipped away.

"Well," Kell said. "A deal's a deal."

"And the price is right," I added.

"My grandfather always warned me about things that come free. He said they always ended up costing too much."

"The wind is free," I suggested.

"That's true," he nodded. "Anyhow, we've got two days to make ready. I don't know how long we'll be gone, but I don't want to just abandon the place. You know anybody looking for a nice house to stay in?"

"M-Master Kell," I stammered. "I – I could keep the place until – until your return."

He looked at me as if I had gone crazy.

"You dolt," he said. "You're coming with me. You think that Wendfala's rook Byrinius let you listen for your amusement? Close your mouth lad. You have a part to play in this, and while I cannot say if that part will be for good or not, your way lies with mine. Unless you absolutely refuse in which case—"

"No!" I cried. "I – I will happily – I mean yes! Yes I will go with you! And yes! I know that Rebecca hates her house. Her mother keeps making babies and she longs for her own place and she'd be a good tenant and . . . "

I babbled on as my heart swelled. There was suddenly before me adventure. Master Kell nearly insisted that I be by his side as he went to slay the Bone-Dragon. What lad of my years could say no to such a calling? Especially after all the stories he had told me on those cold winter nights.

"Looking back on this situation now... little did I know what I was getting into... But back then I was young and ready for some excitement. So, of course I couldn't know the pure hell my master was going to put me through in the coming years. And so, not knowing the full extent of what I was committing to, I happily did what needed to be done to prepare for the journey ahead.

Then I spent the night packing my things. The next day Kell and I visited the chart maker. Kell found the ones he wanted. He offered the man a piece of a broken stem of a golden goblet. The man and I gaped. The fragment was easily worth five times the paper.

"Value is a funny thing," my master said to me on the street. "The gold is precious to the man. His maps will be precious to us soon. Now take this and get us at least five days provisions. I am going to see Rebecca."

He dropped a shard of the gold goblet in my hand. Giddy with wealth I broke the thing into smaller pieces and was myself a master of bartering. I arranged for nine days provisions to be on hand at Nillan's wharf the next day, and still had a thumb slice of gold in my pocket. Kell was pleased.

So was Rebecca. She danced about our cottage as one suddenly set free. That night we broke into the ale and we gave each other a farewell we will both remember until the end of our days.

The next morning Rebecca set us a hearty breakfast and the noon tide found us on the pier watching the gaudiest looking little ship I've ever seen cruise into the calm harbor waters. She was, as the man had said, baby-blue with pink sails and golden yellow rigging. She was coming in slow and steady by a trimmed jib-sail. Many heads turned and I distinctly heard a few snickers.

She was manned by two small sailors. One stood at the helm and the other held the aft mooring line. As the smack neared we had a closer look at the sailor's children. They were girls, and if they were of age as the man had said, they must have been stunted. They stood barely four feet tall, and I thought that all their energy of growth must have gone into their hair. Each wore a braided-tail that ran easily down to their knees, and it was the fiery red of a sunset after a storm. Their skin was a deep coppery tan as if they had lived under the sun their whole lives, and I thought them to have been from the Southern Reaches.

As they came into view I got a good look at the one aft. She was lean but limber. She had true Southern eyes; wide, round and green, and looking like they were in a state of constant wonder. She had such delicate features, and with a slightly upturned nose she was so elf-like that I expected pointy ears. Her stance was solid and strong and she deftly swung me the line. I tied them off at the cleat and the slender craft came to a gentle halt, just as pretty as you please.

The little scamp stood a moment eyeing me. She wore raggedy britches cut off at the knees, and a bulky wool tunic girdled at her skinny waist. She was most assuredly a she, but if she had anything of a womanly figure it was well hidden. She seemed to be sizing me up. Then with a nod forward we both ran to tie up the prow. She danced about the boat as limber as a fairy. She reached her hand to me and I helped swing her onto the wharf. Her hand was like a child's and she whirled smoothly and landed silently. Then, totally ignoring me, she dashed up to Kell. Her sister was already there. They were twins.

"Hello," the one from the helm said so brightly. "I'm Anna."

"And I'm the other Anna," her sister said.

"You must be Kell."

"Uncle told us everything."

"You're going on a quest –"

"—to save a witch –"

"—that's what he said –"

"—is it true?"

"Are we going on an adventure?"

"Where are we going?"

"Wherever it is—"

"—you'll find the *Chaos* a sturdy craft."

"We can take you to the Sands of Time—"

"—and back again."

"All we need is a good chart—"

"—and a star to steer us by."

"We are your servants, Lord Kell. Anna."

"And I'm the other Anna."

Kell burst out laughing. To hear them speak was to hear the same voice, light and lilting like water pouring, and they would have charmed me had I not been so amazed. But then I thought it was a trick, something that they had rehearsed.

"Tell me," Kell said still laughing, "please tell me that you aren't Impa."

As one they frowned.

"We get that—" Anna said.

"—all the time," the other Anna finished.

Then to our shock and amusement they both undid their belts and lifted their tunics to show their belly-buttons.

"Okay?"

"See?"

"Born."

"Not hatched."

"I see," Kell said grinning. "Okay then. Fix yourselves please. So now may I ask how old you are? You seem—"

"I'm thirteen," Anna said with a snap. "And I'm the eldest."

"By two minutes," her twin said.

"Yeah so?"

"So."

"So you could be wrong."

"So maybe I'm not."

"Momma said—"

"She coulda been wrong."

"Well she wasn't."

"How do you know?"

"I was there."

"Well that's just stupid."

"You're stupid."

And as they went on like that I began to understand the name of the boat.

But Kell quickly put a stop to their bickering when he asked them to show us around their fine craft. The two suddenly seemed to glow. We were given a tour of virtually every inch of the boat complete with the history of each decision that went into the making.

But my Master and I were more interested in the workings and the accommodations. The *Chaos* was a tidy craft. Her mainmast was at a slight rake and the mainsail boasted a gaff-sail above. There was a straight up spanker mast dead aft that the Annas declared most excellent for nulling tricky winds. A long jib held the fluttering pink canvas. Below was sparse. There were two bunks and space for bedrolls, a small cook-stove, a handy little tool-bench and plenty of spare cordage and tackle. Kell nodded. The other Anna and I stowed our gear and provisions, while Anna and Kell poured over the charts.

"Can ya sail?" the other Anna asked me.

"I've manned lines," I said. "And I can island hop in a dinghy. But I've never been out on blue water."

"You're honest," she said nodding. "That'll do. Okay, this is the mainsail haul . . ."

And so I was given a primer on the ways of *Chaos* and then we sailed as soon as the tide turned.

When I was younger I dreamed of the romance of the sea. Like all young boys I saw myself cutting a dashing figure on the prow of a brig or merchantman. But I will tell you that the sea is a hard, lonely, and boring place. We lost sight of the Barnacle Atoll before sunset, and as night grew I saw nothing. There was no moon that night and the frosty stars were reflected by the calm waters. Sea and sky seemed to merge. After I got over the initial beauty of the sea, the monotony began to creep in. We had fish for that night's supper, and then Kell sat in the prow and fell into a meditation while the Annas saw to the ship and argued. I was left with nothing to do but listen to their childish blather. I was however impressed with my master's serenity. He didn't seem bothered by the twins childish rants and he almost seemed to glow while he sat motionless with eyes closed.

So the days went. The deeper we sailed into the ocean the rougher the waters were. Sometimes the ship needed quick and lively tending and that was a welcome relief. But mostly the sea was steady and rolling with fair winds. My Master would spend his time either fishing or in meditation. I tried to engage him in conversation. I wanted to know more about our quest. But he was aloof, saying only,

"We shall see what we shall see." Over and over again whenever I asked.

I tried to talk with our crew, but those conversations quickly led to quarrels between them and I was always caught in the middle, ending up the loser and shunned, and Kell would sometimes smirk, even in his meditation. I took to whittling, did my chores and anything else the girls asked, to help keep the peace.

We saw no other boats and no islands, and after our first five days I wondered if we might be lost. But three times a day Anna would look into her sextant, nod happily and mark the chart.

On our seventh day the cool winds became lively. They twisted and ran this way and that and the Annas and I were hard pressed to keep our course. Anna barked one order to me and the other Anna would yell another. I did my best to obey but the more the *Chaos* reeled and careened the more the twins blamed my incompetence. With the winds came a low, thick overcast sky and that day Anna couldn't see the sun to take a fix. The air became chilly. That's when Kell stirred from his reverie.

"I would never think to tell you how to captain your ship," he said. "But my humble experience tells me that your work is futile. Strike your mainsail and trim your jib. The water is steady and the wind can't toss us if there's no canvas."

The Annas looked at one another, then at Kell and then at me.

"Well what are you waiting for?" Anna said.

"Get on the main-haul," the other cried.

The other Anna and I set to the task. Kell went below. But even as the other Anna and I were working the jib the winds calmed. By the time we were finished there was not a stir in the air. That was when the fog began. I hadn't noticed it creeping in until it was growing over us. It merged with the sky and slowly enshrouded the ship. The sea was still.

"What's happening?" I asked.

"Dunno," the other Anna said.

"This is creepy," Anna said.

"It's weird."

"Unnatural."

"Not really," Kell said.

The three of us looked to the man. He had transformed. The simple herbalist was clad in leather armor. The breastplate was the color of oxblood and laced to the back with rawhide. Beneath he wore woven grey chainmail, gauntlets wrapping his arms. His britches hugged his muscled thighs and he wore boots that ran up above his calves, gathering in folds around his knees. Long daggers were sheathed in his boots and short swords crossed his back. And he held his beloved hammer Ashrune in his left hand.

"There is nothing unnatural about magic," he said.

For once the Annas stood speechless. I looked on my Master, and I saw the proud paladin grin a slight grin. He reached a hand into the water and splashed us. We all jumped away from the water.

"Warm water," he said, "and cool air make fog. Or had none of you listened to your elders?"

Anna chuckled. So did the other. So did I.

"The problem is," Kell said. "It's spring. We are in the middle of the Sassty Sea. The air here should be cold."

He waited. We just looked at him like school children

"The air here should not be warm." he said. "Still with me?"

Chapter 3: Yasmeen de LaCroix

"To hell and beyond!" Anna cried.

"To the gates of Eternity," the other Anna echoed.

"How about to the tiller," Kell suggested.

"Absolutely," they said in harmony.

"I'll do it."

"No, I will."

"No me!"

"Tend to your sails."

"There's no wind."

"So?"

"So!"

"Enough," Kell cried. "Put your tongues to better use and blow wind to the sails. Longo, come with me."

I followed my master to the prow. The sea, sky and fog were slate grey and the water was like glass. I watched the gentle ripples roll silently away from the bow. For a long time the only sound was the slow creak of the mast. And then off in the distance we heard someone screaming.

The Annas started to speak but Kell cut them off with a wave of his hand. I heard one of them scurry below, but I was listening more to the ocean. The cries were faint as we drifted, and we strained to find a direction. Sounds can be tricky in the sea fog, but after a time Kell turned his ear, then he pointed and Anna steered.

"The waters are shallow," she said softly.

"I see," Kell answered. "And now I see."

I peered into the mists. Land began to form. Through the shroud of fog I saw low trees, then a short beach. A moment later the ship ground to a halt. The screams were much clearer. We all looked a little to port and Kell nodded. Then there was a long wailing shriek that cut off quick. The silence that followed was chilling.

Quick as quick the Annas leapt off the bow and splashed into the water dragging the mooring line. Kell and I followed, and we soon had the Chaos dragged aground and anchored to a tree.

"You wait here," Kell said to the twins. "Mind the ship."

"No," they said in harmony.

That was when I saw that the two were armed. Anna had a bow and quiver slung on her back while the other Anna wore a belt with no less than six slender throwing daggers. They both held short broad swords.

"Listen," Kell began.

"No," Anna said.

"This way," the other said pointing to the jungle.

And before my master could say a word the two plunged into the undergrowth. Kell just shook his head and we followed. The girls were like vixens in the woods, bobbing and weaving along and under the foliage. A few times I thought I heard them sniffing. They soon struck an ill defined path and urged us on. They disappeared on either side of the trail as my master and I moved low and quiet. Sometimes one of their heads would pop up through the leaves and the other would quickly appear nearby.

As we crept along I started to feel useless. I didn't know what we were heading into but everyone else was armed while all that I had were my wits and my hands. I looked about for a stout branch to use as a club, but all I saw was rotted wood. I wondered what use I might be in any fight.

Then the brush ahead shook in two straight lines. The Annas were on to something. Kell motioned me to hold still. We crouched and waited. Minutes later the twins appeared.

"Pirates," Anna whispered.

"Never seen their likes," the other added.

"Lean like Dorimans."

"But dark like Shorethorns."

"Five of 'em."

"Armed with strange swords."

"They have a prisoner."

"A lady."

"Bound."

"And gagged."

"And they're tormenting her."

The other just nodded wide-eyed. Kell raised his hammer and led. The Annas followed in line while I brought up the lonely rear. Then Kell paused and motioned. The Annas fanned out on either side of him and I crept up to my master then went to my hands and knees to peer into the clearing.

It was as the twins had said. A woman hung by her arms. She was fair skinned with gleaming blonde hair, and she was half naked. Parts of her fine garments were strewn about. Her eyes were shut and she wept while five swarthy men jeered. The men were ugly and hairy, and to me they had weasel-like faces. One of them laughed as he held the point of his cutlass to the shard of cloth above the lady's breast and cut it free, revealing an ample bosom. The woman shrieked.

With a piercing war cry Kell burst forth from the jungle, his hammer swinging. The first pirate froze -- an arrow in his back. As the others turned, one of the men's skulls exploded under Ashrune with blood and bones spraying the others. Kell then whirled, the blade from the hilt of the hammer slashing another pirate's chest open from shoulder to belly. He crumbled with an agonized gurgling. Kell recovered and planted himself before the last two, snarling. The pirates turned ghostly pale, then turned tail and ran. A knife caught one in the back as he disappeared into the foliage. Another arrow whizzed through the leaves.

Kell cut the lady's bonds with the blade of his hammer and caught her in his arms. He yanked away the gag. I rushed forward, grabbing up a fallen cutlass. But even as I did I heard an unearthly cackle.

"Stupid fool," the woman laughed.

And in that moment many things happened.

The woman's eyes glowed. Threads of eerie green light flew from her to Kell's face. My master wailed in agony, his body twitching and thrashing. An arrow flew from the foliage straight at the woman, but she snatched it from the air without ever moving her gaze from Kell. The man who had fallen by Anna's arrow was encased in a sickly light, and before my eyes he transformed into a rat with the likeness of a small man. He snarled, got up on his hind legs, grabbed his fallen cutlass, and then dashed into the woods. I heard the Annas scream. Not a moment later another rat-man burst from the jungle and I was on my back. His forepaws were as big as my hands and he pinned me to the ground. It was strong as a man. Its ugly face within inches of my own, the beady yellow eyes glaring. I cried out and thrashed -- and then my head exploded and I knew nothing.

I woke to a cry of agony that went quickly silent.

My head hung low. I strained to look up. I tried to focus. It was twilight and the night was closing in. A roaring fire lit the clearing. The first thing I saw was my master. He was naked and bound. His wrists were tied with crude hemp across his belly. A thick rough branch had been threaded between his bent elbows and his back, and he was suspended by that stick. His ankles were lashed and pulled up tight, bound to the ends of the pole. His sweat-soaked body gleamed in the orange light and his face was wracked in pain. In the middle of the bonfire Ashrune lay, its leather handle smoldering.

I fared no better. My hands and feet were bound cruelly and I too hung suspended so that my spine was arched backwards. The ropes were so tight I could feel my wrists bleeding, and the pain in my back was growing as I looked to my captors.

There before the fire I saw no beautiful lady, only an old ugly hag, dressed in a fine gown. The woman looked to be over a hundred. Her face was drawn with wrinkles that made sinister shadows. Her hollow eyes were sunken beneath sickly red folds that oozed pink mucus. She had neither pupil nor color, just milky dark orbs with the deathly stare of a shark. The tawny skin on her face was stretched so that the bones of her skull shown through, while her crows feet looked like a mask of deep spider webs. Her teeth were the color of rotten logs and her cracked lips were grey. Over the crown of her head her silver hair was sparse, but from the sides it fell about her shoulders thin and scraggly.

She stood holding a long stick in the fire. The three rat-men were hunched over their fallen comrade, gnawing on the raw flesh of the carcasses. One of them sniffed and then looked to me. Its hideous muzzle seemed to smile and my heart froze.

“The other’s awake Yasmeen,” she said in a high, whiny voice.

“I’ll deal with the pup in good time,” the hag said in a voice that was like dry leather being torn. “As soon as you idiots catch me the bowman.”

“There’s two out there,” one said.

“Three,” another said. “And one’s a warrior elf, and no mistake.”

"I don't care if it's a troop of warrior-elves," the hag said, kicking hot embers at them. "You just better find them if you value your skins."

"Our cousins are sniffing them out," the one said. "The island is small and flat. They have nowhere to hide. It will be dark soon. We'll find them."

Their words stirred some small hope in my heart. The Annas had escaped. But whether the frightened girls had taken to their boat or not I could not know. I clung to the thought that they may be lurking, waiting for the chance to send an arrow or a knife into the hag's neck.

"And what about that?" the rat-man said nodding toward my master.

"That," the old hag chuckled. "That is my salvation."

She then rammed the fiery red point of a hot stick into Kell's thigh. My master grit his teeth and clenched his eyes. His whole body tensed and he let loose a low, agonized wail. If there could have been any vestige of delight in the old hag, I saw it on her face then and there. The rat-men whooped and stomped their feet in joy.

"Scream paladin," the witch taunted as she ground the stick. "Fill your heart with pain and fear. It will make things all the more delectable when the time comes." She cackled evilly.

She then yanked the point out and Kell's flesh smoked. The stench of his burn made me want to vomit when it reached my nostrils.

"Paladin," she said, holding a freshly lit smoking ember under his nose. "You are a prize beyond my dreams. It would be a great thing for me to stand before the great Visalth holding the head of the fool who would seek to slay the mighty one. But it will be an even greater triumph for me to stand once again in the full glory of my youth and beauty."

She grinned as she jammed the end of the stick up the paladins left nostril. Kell didn't scream this time, but his eyes did start to go wild as the witch then took the sharp stick and moved it near his eyes menacingly. She then put the stick back into the fire.

"I know that you won't speak," she said. "You know that if you speak then you admit my claim over you, and once that happens, whatever pathetic power you have will vanish and then even your soul will be at my mercy. Truth be told, paladin, I'm counting on that."

She cackled as she played with the stick in the embers, burning off the blood and flesh on the stick and getting it to glow brightly once again. I saw my master's wracked form tremble, but his face was stern and set. I thought I saw his tense lips just slightly moving.

"Oh I know," the hag went on. "I know that you are strong. I could hold you over the fire and watch your manhood shrivel to cinders and still you would not speak. And I might just do that. Just for fun. But that will come later."

"You see, I understand your sort. You have empathy. You care. And while you care little for your own flesh, you are overwhelmed with concern for others; so concerned that you would risk your quest to save all of your people in the hopes of saving one poor damsel in distress from torment.   Stupid fool."

She turned to him. Her eyes sparkled green, and for a moment I saw the visage of the lady who we had tried to rescue. She batted her eyes innocently, then she turned and the ugliness crept back over her like a swift plague. She stared into the fire and the crackling light reflected in her murky black eyes. Her face seemed to glow with restrained glee.

"Rest assured, you will speak to me. In fact you will beg. You will beg for your companions as I slowly skin them alive before your eyes. My rats will gorge on their guts as they writhe and wail and your heart will burst with compassion, and when your soul is filled with evil thoughts and hate then . . ."

Then she plunged the fiery point into his chest.

"Then I will use the blade from your own hammer to rip out your heart and I will devour it as the last strains of life seep from you. And as I eat your heart I will be restored! Yasmeen de LaCroix will be young again! I will have the power of a holy paladin and my Dark Lord will see my beauty and power and I will take my place among the elite faithful as my master lays waste to all who would stand in our way."

Kell wailed through clenched teeth. He writhed under the burning torment and the hag laughed as she twisted the stick cruelly. The rat-men howled with glee and my heart froze.

"Yasmeen the Beautiful!" a rat-man cried.

"Yasmeen the Terrible," another echoed.

"Yasmeen the Asshole," came a cry from the woods.

A dozen spears rained from above. They sank in the sand and each had a rat impaled. Then arrows flew. The rat-men clutched their throats. Yasmeen was stuck twice but the bolts didn't stop her. She shrieked in rage and stomped her foot. The fire flared and engulfed the clearing in blue and white. The trees caught fire with her cry of fury.

Kell arched his back and thrust his arms. The branch binding him cracked, the fibers of the wood tearing into his flesh. He grabbed a broken shard of wood with his bound hands and charged at the hag with a furious bellow. He caught her square in the chest with the sharpened wood and she fell back with a guttural grunt. Looking around, the rat-men looked like pin-cushions as the woods around us burned.

The Anna's leapt into our midst. In a moment one had Kell's hands and legs freed of the ropes while the other sliced me free with her dagger. Meanwhile the witch Yasmeen had found her feet while Kell grabbed his Warhammer Ashrune from the fire, and I heard his flesh sizzle.

"Kill me then," Yasmeen said crossing her arms before her. "Kill me and put me out of my misery!"

My master needed no other encouragement. He swung the hot hammer with furious blow, fueled by his hatred and pain – and his hammer struck sand. The force of his swing sent him tumbling.

"Missed me," she taunted.

We all looked. The hag stood in the middle of the burning trees. Anna's arrow flew but burned to ashes before it touched her. Kell cried out and ran towards the witch. He swung his hammer but she vaporized and he struck nothing but a burning bush.

"Missed me," the hag sang in a taunting childish voice.

My master roared in rage. He hacked at the blaze until he had opened up a way into the woods. I heard the hag mocking him from beyond. He plunged through. In his rage my master ran heedless. The Annas didn't hesitate. We grabbed my master's armor and what weapons we could and raced after him.

But the island was enchanted against us all. My master seemed always within sight and within reach, but even as we called and struggled forward, he and the teasing old crone would flee from our sight. And all the while the fire raged.

Over time the flames forced us to the beach. The smoke enshrouded us thicker than the fog, and the glow behind us lit the sky with a weird light. We called and called but my master didn't or wouldn't answer. The three of us stayed together, running along the shoreline and ever calling for Kell. We found him standing by the *Chaos*. In the eerie light he looked as one insane, but when he spoke his words were calm.

"Longo."

"Yes master?"

"Be my witness."

"Master?"

"Hear me and remember. I am going to kill Yasmeen. I am going to wrap my hands around her scrawny ugly throat and I am going to throttle the life out of that bitch."

"Yes master." I said, a bit worried that his torments had rendered him insane.

Chapter 4: Of Demons and Angels

It took almost a full day for the *Chaos* to get clear of the hag's enchanted waters. Anna was hard pressed to rediscover our course, and it took another day for us to reach clear blue water and fresh winds. My wrists and ankles had been cut nearly to the bone by the hemp ropes and so while Kell sang chants of healing, the other Anna tenderly bandaged me. Kell's own injuries were cruel, and the burn on his hand was ghastly. He worked his healing on himself also, and it wasn't long before all of us where totally healed... all the physical damage at least.

During the rest of the boat trip a strange thing happened; Kell began to open up. He had the Annas tell their tale, and we were both so amused with their antics and ways that we urged them to tell it again. Kell was particularly tickled with the way they had trapped the spy-rats and so he called them the Cunning Annas. The girls beamed.

Then, sensing Kell's mood, we urged him to tell tales of his own warrior youth, and to my delight he did. I learned a thing or two. I also learned that when my master promised a story, an incredible tale was always told.

But Kell was also aware of my feelings of uselessness. So he cleansed and blessed the rat-men's scimitars, and when he felt sure that all evil had been purged from them, he presented them to me and the Annas. He also gave two long and very sharp daggers.

"These aren't trophies," he said. "These are well crafted weapons from Allieala, a strong, proud land in the southern sea. You must learn to wield them well. *En Garde!*"

The next few days on the lonely sea where littered the clang and clatter of steel as I was taught how to wield them properly. The Annas joined our lessons and no longer was I bored. We made a rotation where two of us would be tutored by Kell while the other saw to the wheel. And so it was that in those days on the Western Ocean I learned how to use swords, daggers, and how to operate a ship.

My master was tireless in his teaching, and when we would stop to eat he would regale us with yet more tales of the war against the Doriman. At night we would sing songs and tell lies. The Annas had some leather workings in their stores, and so the other Anna began to make simple scabbards for our new swords. Kell nodded and directed their fashioning and urged me to learn. Under the girl's guidance I discovered the basics of yet another skill. She was a patient teacher and smiled often at my crude beginnings. The days on that vast expanse of sea were happy, except when I would fall asleep and the nightmares of our encounters with the witch would haunt me.

Then one day things changed.

Anna and I were engaged in battle. My goal was to plant the broad of my blade behind her left knee. She did not know that, nor did I know her aim. She parried and thrust like a rabid weasel. Her sword-work was bold and sure while mine was swift and light.

"You fight like a girl," she taunted.

"So do you," I replied.

"I am a girl."

"Not that I've seen."

"Cur!" she cried as she whirled my blade so fast I almost lost grip.

"Minx!"

I used brute strength to slash and force her to the bulwark. She thought to be clever. She leapt to the rail and then to the hatch cover. But as she jumped I landed my blade home.

"A hit!" I cried. "A hit! Score!"

"Back at ya!" she called bopping my butt.

"Kell!" we both yelled.

But my master was no longer watching. He had been drawn to the prow of the ship. The other Anna started to speak but I held up my hand. I knew my master's mind. He was standing up and holding a line, but I knew that he was meditating, seeking.

"I think," I said softly to her, "that we are coming close."

"To what?" she asked. "What is he looking for?"

"An Angel."

She looked puzzled as we stowed our gear. It was her turn at the wheel and so I stood by her to study what I could. Anna climbed a line up to the top of the boat and peered out into the distance. We all wondered what we would find.

Evening drew about us and with it came high clouds veiling the sun. The sea was ashen grey and rolling. Long, deep swells rocked the *Chaos*, but Kell directed our way straight into them lessening their impact. Water broke the prow and the ship would pound down on the other side of the swell with a thunk. Light was fading when Anna called out,

"Two points starboard quarter!"

The other Anna turned the wheel. The sea splashed my master but he stood unconcerned. I clutched a shroud as we rolled. Then I saw what looked to be a small hill in the distance. It was like a little, bright hill alone in the ocean. The swells crashed about it, sending spume and spray into the air. Kell raised his hand and Anna scampered down the lines as I joined her to trim the mainsail. The ship slowed and as we approached the mound I gaped in wonder.

Here was no rocky rise. Before us sat an Angel on a small flat rock in the middle of the sea. She was naked and sitting with her slender legs crossed and her knees up about her chest. Her arms wrapped her legs and drew up to her face, her hands pressed as in prayer. Her skin was as white as sea foam and without blemish, her golden hair fluttered in the breeze. What I had seen from a distance as a hill were in fact the Angel's wings, folded and pointed above her head like a tall hood, sheltering her from the rages of the sea. They were white with strains of grey running along the leading edges.

But even as we approached those wings opened and fanned. As they did a wave broke behind her sending a stream of white water straight into the air. Our ship ground to a halt, though there was no land beneath us nor rope to moor us. We bobbed in the water before the magnificent being, shocked into awe and silence.

She unfolded her hands and looked up, revealing a beautiful face that was glowing brightly and so fair that neither the Annas nor I could look on it for long without being forced to blink and look away in utter astonishment. Kell stood stead fast.

"I know you Kell," a voice like liquid silver sang. "You seek Gavial, the Angel of Glory."

"I do," my master said.

"How is it that you deem yourself worthy to stand in her presence?"

"I am not worthy," my master answered. "But my cause is."

She smiled and turned her gaze to the Annas and me. I could feel her. It was as though something was peering into my very soul and with that searching came both a sense of delight and one of shame. Her gaze passed me and then I heard the Annas giggle softly as if they had been tickled.

"You are bold, Kell," the Angle said.

“My need is great.”

“And what would you ask of Gavial?”

“A blessing for my quest.”

Laughter like tinkling ice crystals lilted through the air and filled my heart with joy.

“Your heart is good,” she said. “Your cause is just, and your companions wisely chosen. I will grant you entrée; but the rest is up to up to you. But hear this Kell, Gavial will test you.”

“So be it.”

“Vade in pace. Vade cum fortuna.”

And then her wings began to fan. We felt the air about us pulse. The ship rocked and shuddered. Anna and I clutched the mast as we rocked back and forth. Then we were engulfed in a bright white light. It felt as though the ship was spinning wildly as the air about us sparkled. My head was spinning, and a moment later we slammed down back into the ocean. I heard water splash and crash, and then all was calm.

The glittering air melted away and we found ourselves in a watery grotto. The sea rolled calmly toward a shore of white sand that was dazzled with a thousand tiny points of light. Beyond that a yellowy green light glowed from below the earth of two tall statues. The cave rock above us sparkled in the weird lights. The *Chaos* bumped the shore and Anna and I dropped anchor after taking a few moments to collect our wits.

Kell stood silent while looking at the lights before us. Then he shook his head sadly and bade us to don our armor. We obeyed but I wondered why we would go armed into the presence of an Angel. Still, I felt proud to wear my weapons. The other Anna had fashioned a crossed sheath for my daggers that hung on my back, and I was a small shadow of my master as we jumped into the shallow water.

We slogged ashore. The soft sand soon became hard smooth rock. As we approached, I saw the little lights to be small candles set atop tombstones with no markings. They stretched in a vast field making the whole place glow with an eerie green light. There was no path and so we wound our separate ways around the tombstones.

“Why would an angel shrine be surrounded by a graveyard?” the other Anna asked me softly.

All I could do was shrug and be glad that we had all brought our weapons.

We neared the eerie light and marveled at the two huge angel statues. They stood twice the height of the mast of the *Chaos* and were carved of white marble. Who could have made something so magnificent I couldn't imagine. The stone was polished to a luster and there were a myriad of dark vein-like threads throughout the stone. Their wings were spread wide open and seemed to envelope the cavern. They held their arms high and in their hands they clasped bronze swords that crossed above them. Beneath their arms and between their breasts where strange birds with dragon-like wings that hung there suspended silently and drifting slowly in no wind that I felt.

"Curiouser and curiouser," the other Anna whispered. Anna put a finger to her lips and told her to "hush!"

At the base of the giant Angel statues was cleanly cut blue marble stairs that led downwards. We cautiously walked forward and as we came close to the stairs we realized just how huge the Angel statues where. Kell barely reached the stone angel's ankles. Far above the swords gleamed and the bird things whirled slowly. Below we saw a large cavern that had been carved into the grotto. A single narrow set of stairs wound down to a wide landing running all around the base. There were arched doors set in the walls. At the very bottom a pool of green water glowed so bright we had to shield our eyes. In the center of the pool there was a small island, and on that island it seemed to me that a figure crouched.

Kell led as we descended the stairway. Our eyes were dazzled by the light and I hugged the wall to keep my balance. When we had reached the base of the stairs and had our feet on solid ground we were suddenly nearly blinded. Kell raised Ashrune to the angels above and sang a chant in a language I didn't know. Then he charged forward and plunged the head of his hammer into the green water. The splashing sound was more of a shriek – and in that moment the light dimmed.

The bird things above wheeled lower and all about us there were weird stirrings. It took a moment for my eyes to focus, but when they did I saw that the doors we had seen were cell bars. Behind each door where dozens of child-like angelic creatures. They were dancing and clamoring about, many of them reaching their tiny arms through the bars. They seemed to be begging, but they spoke no words. Then I heard something move on the small island in the middle of the water. The other Anna clutched my arm as we gazed across the green water.

In the middle of the island we saw a mighty Angel. She was as tall as my master and wearing glowing golden armor. Her breastplate was inlaid with sparkling emeralds, and her skirting hugged her slender waist and then draping around her firm round thighs. Her yellow hair sparkled like the sun as it draped about her shoulders and wings. Then with shock I noticed that she was chained. A thick iron collar wrapped around her delicate neck and the chain was bolted to the rock pedestal on which she lay.

"This is no shrine." Anna breathed.

"It's a prison." her sister added.

"Hush," Kell said. "She speaks."

But if she did she used no words I heard. Her eyes gazed on my master and she looked as if she were pleading. I watched a golden tear fall from her eye.

"She begs me to release her," Kell said.

"Then you should."

"You must."

"I will," he cried.

In a mighty bound he jumped into the water and swam across the watery moat. He then pulled himself onto the stony pedestal. Kell raised Ashrune above him and then brought it crashing down onto the lock that held the chain – and then Kell wailed as sparks flew from the blow and he was thrown backwards. The Angel reeled in her bonds, her face contorted in pain, and when the smoke cleared the head of Ashrune was cloven in two.

Kell looked at the Angel in dismay, but the woman hung her head and wept.

"Gavial?" he said.

But in response the Angel shuddered as if in pain. My master stood silently, gazing down at the weeping woman, whisps of smoke rising from the shards of his war-hammer.

"There's devilry here," Anna said.

"Mighty devilry, "the other nodded.

"Or," I ventured. "It's a puzzle."

"What?"

But then I heard Kell laugh.

"Of course," he said. "The watery guardian said as much. The Angel would grant her blessing not to brawn but to brain. It will take more than mere strength to defeat Visalth, and I must prove my cunning to be worthy."

The Angel looked to him demurely.

"So," I reasoned. "If there is a riddle here there must also be a clue."

"But there is nothing here," Anna said.

"No writings," her sister said.

"No pictures."

"Just bare walls."

"With cells."

"With cherubs locked inside."

"Poor things."

"Who would imprison you?"

"And why?"

"That," Kell said, "is the question."

The infant angels were clamoring and straining at the bars. The chained Angel looked to them lovingly, longingly, her arms stretched pathetically. I strode to one barred door. The lock was old and rusty. I gave it a swipe with my blade, but other than some rust flaking off, nothing happened. Then the little ones became eager and agitated. Some waved me away while others pointed to the Annas. Their urgings were desperate.

"Me?" Anna said.

"Me?"the other echoed.

The things leapt with glee.

"But Longo is stronger."

"By far."

And then from the island I heard my master laugh. We turned.

"The boy may be stronger," he said chuckling, "but you are innocent. Your strength is in your purity, and that is the mark of an Angel."

The Annas looked at one another, then giggled. The cherubs were becoming agitated.

"But still," I said. "Who would want to lock away an Angel and her children?"

"Don't know," Anna said.

"And don't care," the other added.

"They have the key."
"We strike on three."

"One."

The Annas raised their swords.

"Children?" Kell mulled.

"Two."

The Annas stood and aimed.

"Children!" Kell cried. "Stop!!"

"Three!"

Their cutlasses fell. As one they caught the lock and smashed it to bits. The door flung open and the room was filled with gleeful squeals of freedom.

But as the cherubs passed their jail doors they began to change. The cute little angels morphed into demonic red imps. Their hind legs were like a goat's with cloven hooves. The wings that sprouted were those of a bat and their spidery forearms ended in three-pronged talons. Their ugly dog-heads had long canine fangs, and they had yellow eyes and curved horns.

Two of them harried the Annas and quickly wrested their swords from them. Three came for me and I fended them off, my sword slicing and whistling through the air, but my blade never caught any of the flying devils. Several flew up to the top of the chamber, but as quick as the demons had transformed, the bird-dragons from above swooped to block their escape. Three attacked Kell with the Anna's dropped swords, and the chained angel clutched her legs and drew her wings in around her. The tiny angel's still in their cells made a racket, desperately rattling their prison bars and screaming in high pitched voices.

Then there was a mighty horrible shriek much louder than all the others, and one of the imps above me fell with a knife in its chest. The two others were stunned long enough for me to slice open the belly of another one and cleave the wing off a third, their black blood spattering upon me. Arrows began to fly. Kell had cut one in half in mid-air with Ashrune's blade. When he impaled the other, the third fled away shrieking. Kell picked up the lifeless body of ones of the imps and threw it mightily, knocking the fleeing imp from the air with the body of its brother. The others retreated and hovered above, desperately trying to dodge the Anna's arrows. The bird-dragons wheeled overhead, but didn't attack.

"What the . . . ?" Anna said.

"How the . . . ?" the other said.

"Longo was right," Kell said. "It was a puzzle. But here there are no Angels or cherubs."

He looked down at the chained one. Her wings opened and she clutched my master's feet and looked up at him, pleading.

"Angels are pure," he said gravely. "Angels do not bear children."

And so saying he raised the blade of Ashrune. The silent woman shrieked, but before the knife could strike the Angel of the waters appeared above and stayed his hand.

"You have done well, paladin," she spoke softly. "I am pleased."

"Gavial," Kell said.

The Angel smiled. And with her smile the demons vanished and all was well.

Chapter 5: Galth

The green light in the pool turned a soft, soothing white. The cells around us became small alcoves of devotion and the bird-dragons in the sky above fluttered down into the chamber as beautiful white doves that cooed and circled the Angel. And in that brilliant light Gavial glowed. Where the chain had once been bolted to the floor there sprang a dais of gleaming white marble on which the Angel stood. Kell reverently gathered up the shards of his once mighty hammer and climbed up the stairs to kneel before the Angel in homage.

Her face was still bathed in a radiance that would not let us gaze on her for long, but I saw that she stood far taller than any man. Her wings were outstretched and almost enveloped the cave while her gleaming hair hugged her body like liquid gold. And though I could not look long upon her visage, I could feel her smile.

"Rise now Kell, and gaze upon my face," the divine creature sang softly, but with a holy chordance that I shall never forget. Kell rose, and never had I seen him look so glorious. He was the true picture of a legendary hero. The angel turned towards me and the Annas "You, brave friends, who cower and hide from me, fear not to lift your heads and so to see. For I am Gavial, the Angel of Glory, and you are worthy to be on this quest. Witness now as a Paladin is Blessed, with Strength and Valor Flowing from my Breast!"

To look on an angel is to glimpse the divine. But to look on the Angel of Glory is probably the greatest experience of my life. I was immersed in her beauty and her splendor and her grandeur. My heart was filled to overflowing, and if I were to never gaze on anything lovely again in this world then I would be content. The unworthy son of a poor clam-digging sailor was in that moment and in that room and in her presence exalted to a place among the holy and sanctified. He was pure. He was whole. He was one with the universe. He finally understood what true joy was. While gazing at her magnificence her words came forth like a strange musical symphony of utter purity and wisdom.

"You gaze on me and I do stand above;
this day when you would ask of me a boon
whilst trembling in this holy, sacred room
and trusting life and soul to Angel's love.

"But blessings may be simple as a dove,
as constant as the ever rising moon,
or murky as an ancient cryptic rune,
and oft will leave the blessed a lack thereof.

"So this will be my blessing and my curse;
Men are much like an Angel with one wing.
So seek another with whom you'd fly to death,

and thus with them for better and for worse,
you'll touch my heart and that will truly bring
a blessing from this Angel's lonely breath."

And as she spoke I felt a small, gentle wind that was like a breeze scented with spring flowers. I was borne by that gentle breath forward and I found myself by my master's side, filled with Gavial's blessing.

"Through this portal you must seek your prey," the Angel said. "A journey of a month will take a day. But that will be one day my blessings fade, so tarry not and do not be afraid. Look always forward and never where you've been, and I will be with you behind the wind. The innocents will tarry in my shrine, and I will teach their souls to sing and shine, for my angelic voice will fill their souls, and fanciful tales will loneliness console.

"So henceforth go through this portal, fly to far and distant land, and try your fortune with my blessing in your hand. Be brave to meet the challenge of your quest, return with glory or die like the rest. But if your faith is strong and you hold true, this Angel and her blessing in the wind will be with you."

The Angel of Glory then made a holy sign above our heads, and I felt, and then breathed in a mist of sacred waters.

"*Vade in pace,*" she said reverently. "*Revertar in pace. Et pacis erit vobiscum.*"

With the last of her words a dark hole appeared in the Angel's pedestal. Kell wrapped an arm around me and I wrapped mine around him, and then it was as Gavial had said; together we became like an angel and through the divine portal we flew, the plaintive cries of the Annas echoing behind.

The divine magic propelled us. I felt the earth fall from my feet and it was as if I were looking through a dark glass. I saw the sea far below rolling and churning. I clutched my master while small islands and vast lands passed beneath our feet.

"Look at that," Kell laughed like a giddy school boy. "Just look at that! We're flying Longo. We're flying faster than falcons or dragons, and we're flying on the Angel's magic."

"I hope," I said, "that her magic has a long reach. Look."

Ahead of us we saw a land that was not an island. It stretched before our sight from horizon to horizon. It was a bright sandy land and I saw no trees or shrubs or grass. There was only a vast expanse of windswept desert.

"Galth," Kell said. "Once a proud and mighty realm, it's power stretched to the corners of the globe."

"Master," I mentioned. "A globe has no corners."

"Longo," he replied. "You have spent too much time with the Annas."

"As if I had a choice?"

"Point taken."

"But tell me, tell me of Galth."

"The story is long," he said.

Sand dunes drifted beneath us. Every now and again I saw blackened and charred destruction.

"It is told," my master said, "that the Galth found a harmony between the magic of the divine, the magic of men and the magic of the darkness. They say that the Galth tamed dragons and would entertain Angels and Mystics, Mages and Witches all at the same feasting tables."

"That would have been a feat," I said.

Our journey slowed. Beneath us was nothing but shifting sands. Ahead of us I saw the scant outline of a grand ruin.

"It was," Kell said. "But the Galth became absorbed in the pride of their achievements. They thought that they could do anything, and they set their sights on the Gods themselves. And so began the Dragon Wars."

"But that's a myth," I said chuckling. "Like Methyus stealing fire or Dora lost in the world with her box of poisons. They make lovely poetry but this is the modern world."

"No," Kell said. "Below us is the mythic world, and you are about to plant your feet in it."

The ground rushed to meet us. I screamed as my feet sank to my ankles in sand. I stumbled, tumbled and fell. I rolled head over heels until the soft stuff stopped me. I looked up. Kell was atop the sand dune. He held his arms out to the sky, still clutching his broken Warhammer.

"*Akuste me Gavial*," he cried in a loud voice.

But only the wind replied, batting him with sand. He smiled. Then he looked down at me.

"Get up," he said.

I found my feet. I climbed the dune and there we stared out across the expanse. There were the ruins in the distance, a dark splot against the sand.

"What is it?" I asked.

"Ios Mosley," Kell said, "the place where dragon bones lie aplenty. It was once a strong city, and it was a place of a great battle. That is where one would look to assemble a bone dragon, and that is where Visalth had to have been made."

"But master," I said. "If the White Rook Byrinius spoke true, the battle lies far away in the Realm of the Nine."

"I know. But here is where the Angel of Glory sent us. And so here is where we will meet Visalth."

"But this is crazy," I cried. "We have no food. We have no water. The ruins ahead look to be easily a day's march and I see no wells in between. Nor do I see any dragons. Is Visalth going to suddenly appear? And would the Angel have us do battle with a bone dragon in the middle of a desert?"

"I don't know," Kell said. "Have faith."

As he spoke, the wind stirred and parted the sands before us. The way before them was a clear line to the ruined city.

"And faith will be granted," I said repeating the old charm. "I just wish that it came in the form of food and water."

And so we began our trudge through the desert to the distant ruined city. Long we marched. We rested once, but there was no relief from the heat glaring down from above and pulsing up from below. All the while I wondered why the Angel could not have set us down closer. The heat was infernal. There was no shade to be found and even the dunes cast no shadow. It was as if the sun had stopped in the sky. In time even my master faltered. I used my sword as a crutch and I saw Kell use the broken Warhammer as a staff.

"Master," I gasped as we trudged. "You have magic. Can you not pray some spell?"

"I can create fire," he said plodding on, "if I have something to burn. I can raise water, if water is near. I need a thing to charm a thing."

"Then look, master!"

In the delve between two dunes we saw a small dot of red. We scrambled down, the sand shifting under my shirt. Kell grabbed me to a halt as the sands flowed before us and threatened to engulf the small flower. We crept close until Kell could hold the delicate thing. And then he chanted in words that I did not know. But it was as if the flower knew his words. It shuddered between his hands and then it began to swell. Before my eyes the little red flower grew and matured. It was a tall spindly thing studded with thorns. When it stood to our knees it seemed to me that the plant was a poor source of food. But Kell spoke a small charm, and then with his dagger he sliced away the thorns at the base, grabbed the stem and pulled. The sand gave up a long gourd-like root. Kell smiled. He sliced a handful from the top and cut it in half, giving me a piece. Biting into the fleshy pulp I was suddenly delighted by a juicy mash that was at once sweet, refreshing and satisfying. We both ate greedily.

Then the wind calmed. Kell dashed to the top of the dune and I followed. But even as I reached the crest my master grabbed and dragged me to the ground. He made a motion for silence and pointed. Away in the distance above the shimmering sands I saw a speck in the sky.

"Quickly," he said. "Hide."

We covered ourselves in sand as the dot came nearer, and as it came nearer it seemed to form into a bird. But a moment later I saw that it was no bird. The coarse dark bones seemed to absorb the sunlight. Its long neck and skull were craned and pointed to the ruined city. Its hind legs were tucked up against the hollow ribs and its fore-limbs hugged the bony breastplate as its massive wings swept aloft. Those long wings with stretching bird-like fingers near enveloped the sky above us, but with no flesh or covering to gather the air I wondered that it could fly at all. But I knew that the beast was undead and whatever magic gave it shape and unearthly life could also give it flight. I thought if the mindless creature flapped its wings simply out of memory or habit.

But the eeriest part was the silence. It flew as swift and quiet as an owl at night. And while I thought that I might have heard the wind whistle through its bones as the creature flew directly over us, the thing was silent as a ghost. For a moment my heart stopped as I looked up and through the flying skeleton. But the beast seemed intent on its goal and soared right past us, taking no heed of two cowering humans. I watched as it disappeared into the dark of the ruins.

"It didn't see us," I said almost in awe. "It didn't even smell us. I've heard that a dragon can smell the blood of a human from leagues off."

"A dragon can," Kell said. "But a bone dragon cannot. Nor can it hear. It has no organs for such. It sees, but only things that move."

"You mean . . . you mean that if I stood still in front of the bone-dragon it couldn't see me?"

"Yes. Though how you would get to stand in front of him I don't know."

"Why does it come to this forsaken place?" I asked.

"That I cannot answer," Kell said, standing and dusting the sand from him. "Perhaps this is where he was created and maybe he needs an extra part. Perhaps some magic draws him. We may or may not find out. But here he is and here we are."

"But master? How will you join battle, let alone slay the thing? Ashrune is not whole."

"Gavial would not send us on a task that had no hope. Come. Our way now cannot be so straight. We must hide between the dunes. Its eyes may be dead but they can see far."

Our way was slow, but fortified by the sacred root Kell had found, our way was steady. I longed for the cool and shadow of the night. But it seemed that in all of the time we worked our way the sun hadn't moved.

"There will be no sunset here," Kell said with a chuckle. Galth is cursed. There aren't even shadows."

His words stopped me. I looked down and gave a small cry. Neither of us cast a shadow. I held out my arm, but the sand beneath just blazed with brilliance. What curse could this be? A land with no sunset and no shadows? I quickly caught up with my master.

As we neared the ruined city it began to take shape. It was towering. The ancient architects must have been wizards. Buildings sprang up from tall slender bases and then grew and spread to heights that were dizzying. They sprawled above and there were a series of arches and bridges connecting and supporting them. Everywhere there were spires, tall towers and minarets with graceful collars. As I looked in awe, it seemed to me as though the people who once lived here didn't want to touch the earth. They seemed to want to rise above it.

But the lofty elegance was a shell of its old glory. The city seemed to have been ruined from above and below. Many of the pedestals I saw had gaping holes or huge chunks torn from them as if they had been beset by explosions. The grand structures fared no better, huge swaths of brick or concrete were gone, leaving the iron support work baking in the sun like dark skeletons. Barely a spire above was untouched by whatever had ruined the place, and I saw one peaked minaret had fallen to the ground, its point dug deep into the sand.

"That one looks promising," Kell said pointing up to one tower.

It stood on the edge of the city and I thought it to be a look-out point. There was a rough battlement atop but most of it was damaged. We made our way to the closest entrance that looked fairly sound.

Inside I praised the dark. There was no sunlight here and that was a small blessing. Kell chanted a little and a small glowing light sprang into being above our heads. We marveled at the intricate and ornate stone-work, for even here at a humble entrance the bricks and stone were laid in elaborate patterns that dazzled with both design and faded colors. If what we saw was the norm in this airy city, it must have taken a million slaves a thousand years to lovingly complete.

We found a winding staircase. Kell's light revealed more and more detailed patterns in the building, and even the long dead torch sconces sprouted out of the round walls as if they had grown from living rock. We reached a large room that looked to be purposefully open to the sun. It must once have been a place of leisure, for in the middle was a deep, tiered basin made from colorful polished marble. Weird animal and fish heads leaned down into the basin and I thought that it may of been a pool of sorts. Now it was nothing. Desert dust coated everywhere. Above, an array of long dead, near fossilized plants hung dry, brown and limp. The only sign of any humanity was a jeweled, silver goblet lying on its side on the floor beside the pool.

"Your first spoil," Kell said smiling and tossed the precious thing to me. "Don't get greedy."

From the open room we saw the watch-tower to our right. To get there we had to cross an archway connecting two structures. I had to steel myself from looking down. I hadn't realized how high we had climbed. The arch seemed solid enough, but much of the balusters on either side were broken or simply gone. My head spun.

At the tower we climbed yet more stairs. The Angel's blessing must have indeed been strong, for despite the long trek through the desert and the many stairs in this tower, I felt little fatigue. Then we saw light above and were soon standing at the top. To one side we saw nothing but the shadowless, shifting sands. But on the other side we gazed upon a field of destruction.

As far as my eyes could see, the magnificent city was like one enormous palace, and that palace was in ruins. No building had been spared. Metal frameworks twisted like a myriad of gnarled fingers. Gaping holes were everywhere and huge chunks of rock and stone littered the earth. The desert air shimmered all about and it sometimes looked as if the bones were swaying and waving. The city was lain out in a circle, its flying arches and walkways leading to the center where everything seemed to focus on a grand towering statue, one arm raised to the heavens, a broken sword in hand, and the other arm clutching its heart. The scene of magnificent destruction and desolation was hypnotic.

"Don't move," Kell said, his hand like an iron grip on my neck.

I peered through the haze, the shimmering, shifting wreckage that was rippling. I then saw that two points of iron colored bones near the statue were indeed moving. They were lifting and unfolding like the huge wings of a skeletal bat. The head rose up and there, in the heart of the splendid destruction, was Visalth.

Chapter 6: Visalth

"Scrit," Kell breathed.

The beast launched. With a powerful spring from its hind legs and two beats of its wings it had crossed half the distance to them. I felt the blood drain from my face as that skeletal grin loomed. It's jaws opened wide but no roar came out. In a few seconds it was on us, but a second too late as Kell leapt, and clutching me by the scruff of my neck, we were airborne. The watch-post exploded under the giant jaws and we sailed through the air between the bony wings. I screamed as we arced and fell, but to my amazement Kell and I landed on the ground simply as if we had jumped off a bed.

"Master?" I cried astonished.

Even Kell looked amazed.

"I just . . ." he began. "It was impulse. I just jumped and . . . scrit!"

Bones rushed overhead and that long, sinewy tail swiped a hunk off a nearby building. Rock and dead foliage tumbled about us. Visalth wheeled in the air and turned towards us. Kell grabbed my hand and we again flew up in an arc away from destruction. I heard stones shatter and tumble behind us as the bone dragon tried to catch us. We landed on a tall building spire and Kell leapt again and again throughout the city, always aiming for the largest buildings to jump off of. But the dragon always had us in his sight and though we managed to dodge his wrath time and again, it was clear that the cat-and-mouse game might easily go the way of the cat if this kept up much longer.

"This won't do," Kell said.

We had landed in the open wreckage of an empty room. Visalth circled and took a bead on us. It turned to gain speed and darted toward us, its scorpion tail whistling through the air behind it. Again we jumped, but this time through a gaping hole in the side of the room and down to the sands below.

"Run!" he cried as rocks began to rain.

I saw my master's thinking. We dashed away, under arches and out of sight. We ran through the twisting alleys of debris, and then we ran some more. Visalth roamed above and whenever he came close to view we would go under a rock or wall and freeze. We soon found a tumbled dome that provided great security and we hid. Visalth searched, we knew. Even though we couldn't see him, I could distinctly sense his foul presence every time he got close. Every now and again we could hear stone shattering and falling, but it was clear that he had lost us after an hour of hiding or so.

"I guess," I said as we scanned the empty sky. "I guess he knows that we're here."

"Ya think?" Kell asked dryly.

Just then we heard the sound of a distant tower falling.

"I wonder," I said. "If it might not just try and destroy the city block by block to get us."

"The thing wouldn't have such logic," Kell said. "Its destruction is wanton frustration."

"Do you suppose it will tire?"

"It might," Kell said with a shrug. "But I think it's more likely that it will soon return to whatever it wants here. Remember that it doesn't have much of a brain, but it does have a purpose. If we can find what that is we might find a way to destroy it."

"It was huddled by that statue," I said. "Whatever it wants must be there. I say that we wait until dark and then – oh, right there is no dark here."

"I say that we wait until it loses interest. Then we do some experimenting." Said Kell

"Experimenting?" I asked.

"Gavial's blessing. It's the key to our success I have no doubt." Kell said with a hint of awe in his voice.

"I don't—"

"Hush!" Kell warned.

Through the single window they could see the Bone Dragon soaring above. Its neck was craning this way and that, those death-like eyes searching. Just the sight of it was enough to chill my heart. I had not dreamed a thing could be so massive. And yet, as I gazed up at the magnificent collection of undead bones, I could not see how it could be slain. It had no flesh to tear. It had no heart to bleed. One might crush its skull. But my master's war-hammer was a poor shadow of itself, and even if one might get near enough to land a blow that scorpion tail or those massive jaws would make short work of anyone foolish enough to try.

The bone tail slid from our view and my heart began to beat again. We waited a while but heard no more destruction in the creature's wake. We both sighed in relief. Kell lopped off another hunk of the magic root and we ate and rested for a bit.

Kell then stood up and leapt to a ledge high on the inside of the dome structure. He called to me from high above. He wanted me to try and do the same. At first I thought that he was crazy, but he urged me on and so with a running start I jumped – and I amazed us both. I easily soared almost halfway to the place where he stood laughing. I was flabbergasted, for not only had I bounded as graceful as a gazelle but I also landed as sure footed as any mountain goat.

"You are blessed," he called down.

It took me two tries in earnest to land beside my master and I was astonished. After more experimenting we found that while my strength and agility did not come near Kell's, it was certain that I was achieving some spectacular feats.

"Gavial's grace is according to your ability," Kell said. "But such ability may do much in the end."

"What's your plan?" I asked. "Are we to leap and jump until the dragon falls from exhaustion?"

"Wish it were that simple," he said with a chuckle. "But it's certain that we cannot conquer by strength alone, so we will have to use the things that the Angel of Glory sought in us; we must use our brains. For the moment then we will be like mice. We will furrow through the broken city and discover the monster's lair. There we may find a way to best him."

And so we began. Our way was clear to find, we had seen the dragon in the city's heart and all roads led that way. We did our best to stay out of sight. We snuck through crumbled buildings, sometimes crawling. There were places where we might have climbed up and crossed the arches and causeways that remained intact, but that would have exposed us, so we stayed close to the ground like mice. As we paused in a building to rest my teacher asked,

"Have you noticed something odd about this place?"

"Other than rampant destruction," I began, "a sun that will not set and that casts no shadows, and a pretty nasty dragon, no. Have you?"

"Yes. This was the heart of the Dragon Wars. So . . .?"

"So," I mulled, and then it hit me. "Where are the dragon bones?"

"Indeed. Where are they?"

We zig zagged the ruined city until we found a small, nearly unblemished building whose wooden door had long crumbled off its hinges. Inside we climbed a winding staircase to the top of the tower. From that circular battlement we peered through arrow-slits and the sight I saw was unreal.

I looked down at what was once a proud city square. It was nearly two acres across and almost as wide. There were broken off statue pedestals and what looked like roads paths that I imagined filled with the city people who once lived in this place. But all that was gone, and strewn about the entire grounds were thousands upon thousands of bones, some huge and some small, some bleached and some near rotten brown.

In the center of it all stood the immense stone statue of the ancient warrior, his broken sword raised to the sky and his hand clutched to his heart. At the foot of the figure the ground was clear and there we looked down at an amazing sight; the bones of a nearly whole dragon lay prostrate before the statue. From head to tail and from wingtip to wingtip the skeleton sprawled as if in homage.

Then I heard a clatter off to one side, and there was Visalth. The monster was rooting like a rat through a giant pile of bones.

"What the hell?" I breathed.

"I think," Kell said. That our friend is trying to build himself a playmate."

"B-but he can't," I said. "He is undead. He has no magic. He can't animate that pile of bones."

"And yet he is very intent on doing just that."

"What do we do?"

"We stop him."

"How?"

"You see the ribcage on his playmate?" Kell asked.

I did and nodded. Visalth had found a near entire spine with the protruding bones.

"That," Kell said "Will be the safest place for you. And if all else fails, go for the wishbone."

"What?" I stammered.

But he didn't answer. With a blood-curdling cry he leapt from the top of the tower and sailed through the air. Instantly Visalth rose and launched at him. The bone-dragon roared a silent roar as my master plunged and landed on the lifeless skeleton's skull at the base of the statue. Visalth reared in midflight. Kell raised Ashrune and the creature flapped and flailed as if it were in pain. Kell sank the broken peen of the war hammer onto the ancient bone. Visalth flapped and thrashed in the air. It sent its whip-like tail at my master, but Kell quickly disappeared into the skull's eye socket. Visalth went mad in the air, flapping and flying as his tail whistled through the wind and did nothing.

Then I understood. The skull of its brother was precious, and though he could have laid waste to Kell then and there, my master's death would have been too costly. I silently cheered as Visalth hovered then circled.

It was a standoff. My master's wounded weapon could not harm the ancient skull. But the ancient dragon would not harm the head of its creation. But watching its slow and studied flight around and around I realized that the dragon could out last my master. The Angel's blessing was waning and so I didn't think. I leapt.

I landed in the sand beyond the dragon's reach but within his sight. Immediately the boney tail plowed the earth before me. My mission was accomplished. Visalth had me in his deadly stare. I ran and dove under a stone overhang and the tail slashed. Ancient stone exploded above me and I hit the dirt with a thud, rock shards shattering about me.

I braced for another blow, but none came.

I looked. I lay under the toes of the grand statue. Visalth had taken a chunk out of the ankle and it was flying away. It reared and flew as one pained, and I marveled.

But just then Kell burst from the jaws of the inert skull. He leapt and caught Visalth by a rib. The dragon twisted and writhed in the sky as Kell beat on him from within. Visalth rolled and its scorpion tail tried to stick Kell from inside itself.

I watched the weird battle. Kell climbed the ribs to the creature's spine, but the dragon wormed and flexed and wiggled to expel the invader, swooping and climbing and diving until Kell crouched just under the thing's neck vertebrae. I thought that surely from there my master might be able to deal a crushing blow, but that was not Kell's goal. He climbed up as if to straddle the spine and I cringed, for surely that would simply be asking for that snaking tail to slice him in two. I watched from below as the dragon flew by. Then, as it turned its ghastly head, Kell leapt off his quarry and onto the statue looming above. Visalth raced by, its gaping jaws open in a silent roar.

From where I crouched I could not see my master, so as the bone-dragon sailed on I quickly scurried from cover and made a mad dash through the sand to dive between the inert skeleton's ribs. Visalth saw, turned, and hovered above me. The pointed spear of his tail darted here and there about above me, but it seemed that the monster had no clear shot at me and so held back.

Looking up I saw my master nestled in the hand of the statue. Kell was kneeling, his back to the beast, and it looked to me as if he were chanting. A moment later I saw a thin whisp of smoke rise.

Visalth flew up and over, rolling and somersaulting madly in the sky. It was confused. It would swipe at the statue, but it was clear that he was as loathe to injure the marble warrior as he was to harm his fellow bones. Then it dove toward me, but I stood stock still and it saw only the futility of its assault. It would then rise in the air to strike at Kell, only to roll his head, his maw gaping in silent frustration.

Kell and I were safe for the moment. But how long could those moments go on? The dragon tried to land on the statue, but its hind claws found no purchase, and the massive creature fell away. Once it landed beside me, its hideous face not yards away. It craned its neck and opened its jaws, and whether that was to frighten me or to try to roast me with fire it did not have I would never know. It succeeded in terrifying me, but it had not even a warm breath. It launched away again in blind aggravation.

And then the wind stirred.

Warm air rose up behind me. It ran through the massive bone cage of the almost assembled dragon and swirled the dust at the base of the statue, picking up flakes that sparkled. The glittering wind climbed up the statue and for a moment enveloped my master and then it crept up and up the statue until it encircled the top of the stone warrior's head. The sparkling mass whirled there for a moment like a halo, and then I watched in astonishment as the marble eyes of the statue opened.

Those terrible eyes gazed down at the layout of bones beneath it, a golden streaming light that enveloped the whole skeleton. And then the bones began to stir. I was frozen in horror as bit by bit, chink by chink, the joints of the skeletal dragon began to magically come together. They were fusing with some unholy magic and I heard the rippling of the spine above me stir with a new animation. The wings flexed. The neck rolled and the head began to lift.

My dread overwhelmed me. Visalth was swooping and soaring in victory as its brother began to rise from the desert dust. And despite my terror, my mind went straight to my master's words even as my hand gripped my sword.

"If all else fails, go for the wishbone."

With the cry of a berserker I did not know I had in me, I leapt toward the delicate V-shaped Wishbone and clove it in two as if I were slicing through water. The creature's wings collapsed and its neck and head plowed into the dirt. The body began to thrash, but even as I looked for my escape I saw a wonder.

Kell was shrieking down toward the newly animated and flailing dragon. Riding on the golden light from the statue's eyes, he dove down, holding Ashrune with two hands over his head – and the mighty war-hammer was healed and bathed in a powerful glowing light. In a flash Kell came down and smashed his newly blessed Warhammer into the dragon's skull. It exploded into thousands of pieces, a few digging deep in my side.

Ignoring the pain, I raced from the crumbling disaster and looked up. Visalth was startled. He hung in mid air as he watched his triumph disintegrate before him. But then its dead eyes seemed to turn to cold murder. It gathered himself and plunged straight for Kell. But my master was well ahead, for even as Visalth dove Ashrune was launched into the air to meet him, and with a snap and a mighty crack, one wing was severed from the body and the bone-dragon's wrathful assault became frantic as it crashed hard to the ground, shattering many bones near the ruin of its brother.

But Visalth's rage was not quelled. Even wounded and near paralyzed, his tail and head were still viciously flailing at my master and me. We leapt out of its deadly reach and watched its impotent frenzy.

"There will be no more bone dragons from this place," my master said.

And so saying he strode to the base of the mystical statue and Ashrune shattered away a large chunk of the leg. Another blow and the marble statue teetered. And with a third mighty blow the footings burst asunder and the grand form began to fall. Kell easily stepped aside as the statue smashed to the ground, crushing what was left of the cursed undead bone dragon.

But before we could taste success the warm wind whirled around us and we both heard the echo of the Angel's voice;

". . .and oft will leave the blessed a lack thereof . . ."

We turned from the devastation. Kell gripped the newly healed and magnificent Ashrune and hefted it aloft, giving thanks for the victory this day. We then launched into warm wind of the angel and high into the sky. And so, carried by the warm Angel's wind and the power of the healed and mighty hammer, we sailed away from the ruins. We crossed the searing desert, past huddled remains of Galth's outlands and out and over the sea.

Swiftly we left the accursed lands and swiftly we were back in the mortal world. The sun was low in the west and Kell found a star to guide us. My master pointed Ashrune and its power flung us faster. The waters below whizzed by at a dizzying speed, the wind rushing in our ears louder than any dragon's roar.

We indeed needed that speed, for even as we flew like birds through the air, I began to feel a weariness creep over me. My limbs ached and I clutched at Kell. I saw his arm sag with the weight of his weapon. Then the wind behind us began to cool and our flight faltered. I heard Kell groan and felt his body tense as he strained and fought for every ounce of the blessed magic. But time and tides tarry for no man, no matter how desperate his plight nor how worthy his cause. And so we fell toward the wine-dark rolling sea.

"I have failed you," my master sighed.

"No master," I cried. "You need to..."

We hit the ocean hard.

Chapter 7: Of Angels and Demons

The waters were rough and I floundered, the waves filling my mouth with salt water. The sun was all but set and the rollicking waves cast deep shadows. I called for my master but a slap of salty water made me choke and sputter. My boots filled and were dragging me down. The weight of my weapons made swimming impossible and I strained just to keep my head above water. My strength was fading, but the sea was unconcerned. I sank below the water, my heavy boots leading the way.

Then I found myself filled with a strange calm.

I had had a good life. I had learned love. I had seen wonders and magical marvels. I had gazed upon the face of an Angel, and I had helped a great warrior destroy a great evil. I was in a sort of peace as the waters drew me down. I might die, but because of me and my master, many in the Nine Realms would live, though they would never know the tale. Still, the Angel of Glory would know and that thought comforted me. I ceased my struggles and sank into the bosom of the sea.

It was quiet there. It was warm and dark. I was floating. I was not sinking, but rather I hung adrift in the silence. After a time my lungs wanted air and I knew that in a moment, maybe two, my body's instincts would overcome me and I would gulp in the water and that would be the end.

In my haze I thought that I had gone delirious for I saw a woman approach me. She was naked and had such lovely, creamy skin. Her brown hair flowed all about her as if it were caught in a vortex. She smiled at me and her azure eyes sparkled. I thought it might be a kindly hallucination, a sort of final shard of the Angel's blessing. I was tickled and almost laughed aloud as the vision wrapped her arms around me and kissed me full on the lips. I was neither stunned nor embarrassed, but held the dream-like woman and kissed her back with all the warmth she had given me.

And then there was a miracle.

My aching lungs were suddenly filled and the woman felt as warm and solid and real as could be. She pulled away from me, the divine kiss still warm on my lips and she smiled, and even as she pulled away my body was encased in a layer of air. It was as if a shimmering second skin of air had enveloped me, I became like a bubble of life in the ocean depths, and wrapped in that magical bubble I freely breathed in a place where I should have drowned.

My beautiful Nereid smiled again, a smile of joy and she took my hand. We swam on and to my astonished joy she brought me to my master. Kell floated in a silvery bubble of air as well, grinning and laughing a silent laugh. The woman took his hand in her other and through some power of hers the three of us began gliding easily through the ocean as quick as elegant fishes.

Our way was swift and our line was straight. I saw many wondrous marvels in that watery realm, things I would strain to recall and log later on. But my mind was on the end of our quest, and I yearned to thank the Angel of Glory and give her all due homage. I longed to be back aboard the *Chaos*, listening to the Annas bickering, content to sail for home.

We continued onwards for many hours before our watery savior dragged us up and we broke the surface of the sea in the calm cove before the Angel of Glory's grotto.

Suddenly a loud cry shook me from my reverie. "Kell!" a beautiful woman cried. Then she rushed forward and into the ocean, swimming to us and flinging her arms around my master's neck, kissing him long and deep, right there in the water. "You saved me."

"You saved me Wendfala," my master said as soon as she let him speak several minutes later.

"I rescued you," she said, "but only after you destroyed Visalth. When his cursed life was destroyed so were the chains that bound me. Even as we speak, his armies are panicked and fleeing. You are a hero, Kell, and I will see that the whole of the Nine Realms know of your great deed!"

"Don't forget my comrade," he said nodding to me. "My apprentice—"

"An apprentice learns a trade," she said.   Her eyes scanned me thoughtfully. "Here is a disciple, for truly I see great deeds in both of your futures."

She kissed me on the cheek and I blushed.

"I just hope that's a wish," Kell said as we swam, "and not a prophecy."

I was tired and I was weary and I so wanted my master's hope to be true. But that was not to be, for even as we waded up onto the soft sand shore of the Angel's grotto, we saw that things were not right – not right at all.

There was no light. The hundreds of little candles on the gravestones were all gone out. We paused on the shore. The glow from Gavial's chamber was dark. Wendfala waved her arms and spoke a word and the cavern was lit as if by the sun, and what we saw stopped my heart.

Every tombstone that surrounded the place was on the ground, as if some burst had exploded and laid them low. The two giant statues that guarded the chamber were broken. One had been shorn in half and the other's head and wings were gone. But beyond that destruction and to my own horror, the *Chaos* was surged up against the grotto wall, its mast snapped and the rigging laying about in a tangle.

"Anna!" I cried as I raced blindly toward the Angel's shrine. "Anna!"

But there was no reply. Kell and Wendfala caught up with me and we reached the top of the stairs together. At the top I stumbled and almost fell in. Kell just managed to hold me back and we gaped down at the abyss.

Where once Gavial had tested us and greeted us and finally blessed us, there was nothing but a deep round void that seemed endless. As if some force had reached up from beneath the earth and tore it away, the Angel's chamber was no more. In its stead was a yawning dark chasm lit only by Wendfala's magical flame.

"Anna!" I screamed into the darkness.

"What power on this good earth could do this?" Kell said in quiet amazement.

"No power on earth," Wendfala answered. "We must leave here. My heart doesn't feel good and we must leave now if we want to live."

"No," I cried, and then shrieked long and loud into the abyss again, "Anna!"

Someone clutched my shoulder but I shook it off. I stood in despair listening to my own echo.

"We must go," Wendfala said. "There is nothing here that we can do, and if the powers that did this returns--"

But even as she spoke a single soft word drifted up from the depths.

"Longo . . ."

I sank to my knees gazing down. A small vapor of mist appeared. I craned to look as it rose, and as it rose it began to take shape and the form it took was,

"Anna?" I said.

"Longo," the misty apparition smiled. "Would that all of your kind was as simple as you."

"Anna . . . what?"

"Is that what you call the child," the vision said. "She wouldn't tell me her name. She has this silly notion about names holding power. So quaint. Still, the body is young and fair, and it feels so nice."

"What have you done with the – "but before I could finish Kell slapped me aside.

"The Angel," my master finished. "What have you done with Gavial?"

"And who are you?" Wendfala demanded.

"Questions, questions," the misty thing answered. "But that's alright. I will answer because I want you three to tell the world who it is that has the power to enslave an Angel."

"Then tell us," Wendfala cried. "Who are you?"

"I am as I am," the voice of Anna said. "I am the mind bending Mistress of the nightmare that witches and wizards would never dare dream of. I am she who terrifies the undead and who haunts the thoughts of the gods themselves, and I am she whose name they will not speak.

"Go away then demon," Wendfala goaded. "For truly there is no good here."
"There surely is not." The mist laughed spitefully. "I am the right hand of the idiot who thought he could use my pet dragon to conquer your pitiful Nine Realms. While your cunning led to my pet's defeat, my minion's failure is also my victory, for while your holy paladin was distracted, I saw into Kell's mind and knew it blessed."

"So now I know how to defeat you Kell," the voice said with a sneer. "Your foolish quest may have defeated my dragon, but that bundle of bones was just a pittance of my powers, and your pathetic waste of an Angel's blessing led me to the shadow of her wind... and so here I am thanks to you.

"And you Longo," the vision smiled. "Longo the Simple. You go forth and tell all that you meet of all that you have seen. But also tell them this; tell them that I am she who will conquer all. Once you came to this place for an Angel's swift blessing, but you will leave now with my slow curse. So hear my curse now simpletons, and hear it well.

"For ninety-nine nights and one hundred days your world will know nothing but a driving, vengeful rain. Waters will rise and islands will sink. In the lands that survive crops will rot in the fields and in the stores, and after that a famine the likes of which your world has never known will come. Behind that famine will come plague and pestilence, and the peoples of the world will war among themselves until nothing is left but a ragged bunch of bedraggled desperates who I will enslave into my service.

"So go now, Longo the Simple. Go with your friends and tell the world that I am everlasting and that I am patient. And tell them to be afraid. Go!"

And so saying the misty vision of Anna vaporized.

"Kell," Wendfala said softly. "I think . . . I think that we should be afraid."

"I think," Kell said, "that whatever that demon was, it missed something."

"What?"

"The other Anna," he said. "I'm sorry Longo, but that's why I stopped you from talking – before you could say *the Annas*. That thing knew only of Gavial and Anna. She didn't know that there were two of them."

"That means," I said slowly. "That means that the other Anna . . ."

"Could be anywhere," Wendfala said. "Angels are powerful, and it could be that in Gavial's desperation she hid the child."

"Then we must find her," I said. "She's the only one who could tell us more about that wicked being."

"The girl could be anywhere," Wendfala said. "We must look for guidance. The girl might give us a story but we need wise counsel. If that wraith spoke anything near true, then we must seek Gavial's sisters."

"Anna saved our lives," I cried. "We must look for her."

"Anna is one life," Wendfala said. "I am sorry for your little friend Longo, but a thing that could capture an Angel is a thing to be feared and fought. We are puny in the light of that power and so we must look for greater help."

"First," Kell said. "We must look to the *Chaos*."

My master walked down the beach and across the fallen tombstones. As he walked, a silvery noise began to dance about the grotto. We looked to the mouth of the cave and it began to rain.

The End of Book 1

Be Sure To Check Out Book 2: The Sands of Time: Available Now!

Chapter 1 : The Witch Harpy of the North

There are stories still being whispered among the people of Theugua. Stories told about creatures hiding in the darkest corners of the world. Stories told about magic that could turn good and honest men against each other, stories about deeds that are darker than even the moonless night sky. Even so, men are quick to forget. Soon those hushed stories became nothing more than children's tales told in times of peace.

For Ornsell son of Krull, that was always the case. The stories of the past were just legends that would never come to pass. He decided to start his day early and head straight into the woods to check the traps he had set the day before. As he proceeded along at a brisk pace, getting back home in time for supper was his only concern. Handling his axe with ease, he set off towards the forest. He was also planning to cut some firewood that would last him and his son, Vygarast, for a week on his way back home.

Day excursions into the forest west of Midvein were ordinary for the village people. Though the winters up north of Theugua tended to be harsh and unforgiving, the men and women of Midvein were tough. They knew that the best way to survive the cold winds of the north was to be prepared for anything.

The morning dew had covered everything in the forest with a sparkling veil under the rising sun. Ornsell had his hands folded in front of him on his chest to try and keep himself warm. Taking a deep breath every five strides or so, he soon found himself deep in the woods and his exertions made the chill less now.

Winter mornings are the best remedy for an old man's head like mine. This is as good day as any to explore deeper into the forest, how many good days yet until I can't take a walk into the forest without needing Vygarast to help me? He laughed on the outside at the thought of being helped through the forest.

His eldest and only son was destined to be a Bard, one trained by a living legend, Lanarast the Bold. Being around to take care of him was not in his son's plans. *So be it!* He laughed it off. *If Vygarast's fate is to sing in the kings' courts and charm women with his voice for the rest of his life, then so be it.* However, a sudden frown and flush of emotion betrayed that thought. Memories of his life as a Bard (an amateur one that it was) kept interfering with his expectations for his talented young son.

You can't be jealous of your own son Ornsell. He has talent where you only had luck to rely on. Just get over it! With a quick shake of his head, he kept on heading deeper into the forest, sometimes choosing to follow the forest path, other times getting away from it. The forest was beautiful and full of life despite the chill. However, Ornsell could not get his son out of his mind. Lost in his own thoughts he ventured deeper into the woods. It was only after hearing a twig snap behind him that he jerked suddenly aware, his thoughts alarmed. He turned around only to see the dark shadows cast by the trees dance around him on the ground. Even if he couldn't see it, something felt wrong to him.

Bears are still asleep this late in the winter and it's too early into the day for the wolves to hunt. Normally, Ornsell was not a man who fretted over a dry twig snapping, but he couldn't shake the feeling that something, or someone, was following him.

A seasoned soldier, one matured in the last war of the Horizons, Ornsell wasn't afraid of any man bearing a sword, nor even some who cast magic. Nature was his only concern and by paying his respects to the Great Mother every spring, he didn't have anything to be afraid of. No, no matter how many times he thought about it, still something just wasn't right.

I hope Skann's boys are not in the mood for one of their pranks again or they're going have a day's worth of bottom ache when I finish with them. Those kids smell trouble from afar, especially since their father doesn't give them a good beating when they deserve it. Still, Ornsell went on, despite knowing quite well that a kid's prank would not leave such a vile sense in the back of his mind and that they would not dare venture this far into the forest alone.

Looking around, Ornsell suddenly realized that he had no idea where he was. The sun's bright rays barely crept between the leaves of the mighty evergreen and oak forest. Shadows were dancing as grey clouds passed above the thick forest. Cold sweat started to run down Ornsell's spine.

Whatever is following me can't be good. His left hand instinctively rested on the handle of his axe. Then he slowly pulled it out as his heart pounded fiercely in his chest. His brown eyes quickly examined his surroundings, trying to make out what had made that noise. Unaware of what was chasing him, he decided to follow his instincts and run. His warrior's sense of intuition, honed in the heat of the battle, was the only reason he was still alive after all of these years. The few times he didn't hear them, or he ignored them, he ended up in the back lines, limping and nursing his injuries.

Ornsell saw a break in the forest and took off, crashing through the forest for a full ten minutes, unable to spot anything in the dark behind him. The rustling of the fallen leaves being squashed under his boots became more apparent, and a few cracking twigs that he didn't break sent him jumping behind a large giant oak tree, noticing a terrible pain in his right ankle as he did so. His mind wasn't sure that something was actually following him, but his gut kept shouting a warning. *You have to run, old Orn, you have to run and hide!* With his right ankle aching badly he knew that the only way to get out of there alive was to either hide or fight.

He ran into a clearing amidst the dark woods. Ornsell knew that this place was his best chance for salvation. He was never one for hiding, especially not when he had a perfectly good axe in his right hand and solid ground beneath him. But he knew not to ignore his gut, so he brazenly ran towards the golden light of the still rising sun. Ornsell was sure he could sense the freezing breath of some vile creature on his neck. With desperation, Ornsell dove into the illuminating circle of the glade, landing roughly into a throng of black twigs and unearthed roots.

Gasping, he quickly stood on his feet once again. The warmth of the sun falling on his shoulder was relieving. Hungry for air, he looked around, searching for a good reason to explain his panic. *What is going on inside these woods?*

When he heard the flapping of the wings, it was already too late to do anything about it. The moment the talons of the creature penetrated his shoulders the forest echoed with his pained scream.

Dropping his axe, Ornsell could do nothing but bare the excruciating pain of his whole body being carried aloft by some large feathered monstrosity through the gap in the forest. As they rose he grabbed desperately at the clawed talons, but he could barely move his arms the brutal grip was so tight. HThe talons sunk in even deeper and then he passed out. Moments later, Ornsell regained his senses only to find himself released from the grip of the monster and falling on the outskirts of the forest, close to his home. His steep fall was painful, knocking the wind from him. The flapping stopped with a solid thump on the ground next to him.

"It has been years since the last time I saw humans. You haven't changed a bit, still fragile and puny, like maggots swinging their tails to the sun." A woman's twisted voice boomed behind him. Unable to talk, Ornsell tried to keep up by examining the talking creature. "Oh, you're still conscious. That is commendable. You're lucky that I'm not here to kill you, human, although you'll soon wish I had. I'm here to deliver a curse to you and let the world know that we're back. The legends have come back to life, and soon every nightmare will haunt you whilst you still lie awake without slumber."

Ornsell heard the hoarse voice of the monster mumble in a language unknown to him. His eyes were barely able to focus on the monster's figure; hands full of dark feathers, long feet that ended in sharp talons, pitch black eyes. The legends were true when they spoke of dark creatures that once roamed the land of Theugua. This creature was one of the worst, a harpy witch.

Her feathered hands moved in unison, her words giving a hazy rhythm. The dark magic of those creatures needed no instrument or guidance. Sounds coming from the darkest corners of his mind made a crude melody to accompany them. Being a Bard in the past, Ornsell knew something of magic. Whatever magic this creature had done to him seemed bad indeed.

She took a step forward and looked over him. With one of her black feathers, she touched the wound in his back. A drop of scarlet blood glistened on the feather when she stepped away. With a sharp pull, she uprooted it from her body and let the droplet run all the way to its root. When the dark red sparkle dropped to the earth, a feeling like fire started spreading from Ornsell's legs and up his back. Cackling like some insane parrot, the harpy witch swiped him across his cheek with a sharp talon then vaulted into the sky, cackling as she flew away into the distance.

His feverish thoughts ran wild. The burning feeling in his legs and back was getting worse with each passing second. Pain usually sharpened his senses, but the throbbing pain just clouded his mind. *I have to get home. I have to. . . ,* but he was unable to complete that thought. His body was stubborn like most people from Midvein, with a strong mind. Blinded by pain and rage, he thought of his family as he crawled towards his home.

Vygarast chortled as he escorted young Noelene to the mansion just outside of Midvein. He was with a beautiful young girl who was pleasant company for him. Noelene was a sweet servant to the local royalty and was destined to live and die under the command of her mistress. But even though her fate was already known, Noelene always shared her sweetest smile with everyone.

The young Bard knew that he would soon complete his training under master Lanarast (that old geezer was always boozing and piping) and that he would soon venture out of Midvein to see the world. However, Noelene was still a great pleasure to be with. The young woman was quick to complain that she imposed on him, but every time they arrived in front of Vygarast's house, she stopped and insisted they stand together to say their goodbye.

"Don't worry sweet Noelene. My father is a grown man and can stand a few hours without my company."

She blushed as Vygarast approached her and put his hand around her shoulders. "But my mistress always sees us together. I can't let her think that something is happening between us. It would dishonor her and Lady Aderfell. I can't do that to her."

Embarrassed, she lowered her eyes and tried to get away from Vygarast's sweet but firm grip. But the young man was charming and his bright green eyes had long cast their net to catch Noelene's heart. "Don't worry. If that ever happens, I will restore your honor by asking your hand in wedding. You know that I'm an honorable man, one who always keeps his word, right?"

The blond girl did not answer. Her eyes were wide open, her hand stretched, pointing towards Vygarast's house.

"What is going on Noelene? Is everything okay?" Before he was able to complete his thought, Vygarast looked towards the house himself.

He strode as fast as he could, almost losing his footing a couple of times along his way, hurrying to his father's motionless body. He was a bloody mess on the ground and Ornsell growled like a wounded animal when Vygarast got to him.

"Father! Father, what's wrong? Father, who did this to you?"

With great pain and with the last of his immense strength, Ornsell whispered in an agonized voice: "...harpy witch..."

Check out the rest of the story in book or audio book format on my website: <u>www.LordHartRules.com</u>

My Other Books and Audio Books

For A Special Treat, check out my
AUDIO BOOKS

Thanks for reading!

If you enjoyed this book a nice review would be greatly appreciated.

Check Out all My Books and Audio Books
at: www.LordHartRules.com